Fish for Dinner

Written by Jo Windsor

Illustrated by Brent Chambers

Mom went fishing.

Mom's fish

"Fish for dinner!"
she said.
"I like fish."

Dad went fishing.

Dad's fish

"Fish for dinner!"
he said.
"I like fish."

Grandma went fishing.

Grandma's fish

"Fish for dinner!"
she said.
"I like fish."

Grandpa went fishing.

Grandpa's fish

"A big, big fish
for dinner!" he said.
"I **love** fish."

Mom and Dad and
Grandma and Grandpa
went for a swim.
"We like swimming,"
they said.

The seagulls went fishing.

"Fish for dinner!"
said the seagulls.
"We **love** fish!"

A Mapping Chart

Mom

Dad's fish

Dad

Grandpa's fish

Grandma

Mom's fish

Grandpa

Grandma's fish

Guide Notes

Title: Fish for Dinner
Stage: Early (1) – Red

Genre: Fiction
Approach: Guided Reading
Processes: Thinking Critically, Exploring Language, Processing Information
Visual Focus: Mapping Chart

THINKING CRITICALLY
(sample questions)
- What do you think this story could be about?
- What do you think you need to go fishing?
- Why do you think people go fishing?
- Why do you think Grandpa looks very pleased with himself?
- What do you think they should do with the fish before they go swimming?
- Look at the seagulls on page 11. What could they be thinking?
- Look at pages 12–13. How do you think Mom, Dad, Grandma and Grandpa feel?
- How do you think they feel at the end of the story?
- What do you think they will do about dinner now?

EXPLORING LANGUAGE

Terminology
Title, cover, illustrations, author, illustrator

Vocabulary
Interest words: seagulls
High-frequency words: the, went, by, said, she, I, like, in, we, he, for, big, a, and, they
Compound words: seagulls

Print Conventions
Capital letters for sentence beginnings and names (**M**om, **D**ad, **G**randma, **G**randpa), periods, exclamation marks, quotation marks, commas